W9-CIH-177

GLOSSARY

bar mitzvah – a Jewish coming-of-age ceremony for a thirteen-year-old boy

bat mitzvah – a Jewish coming-of-age-ceremony for a twelve- or thirteen-year-old girl

Hashem – God

Kotel – Western Wall (or Wailing Wall) in Jerusalem

mezuzah – a small box with parchment inside placed on the doorpost of a Jewish home

mitzvah – commandment, often translated as "good deed"

niggun – wordless melody

Sh'ma Yisrael – literally means "Hear, Israel," a prayer recited by Jews in times of trouble

shtetl – a small Jewish town in eastern Europe

tish – the Yiddish word for table

For my parents, Mara and Marek, whose resilience and courage showed me that there is light, even in darkness.
–F.L.

For the generations that teach and inspire, for my mother Sophie and my daughter Rachel.
–S.B.

Designed by Andrew Watson

Intergalactic Afikoman
1037 NE 65th Street, #167
Seattle, WA 98115
www.IntergalacticAfikoman.com

Publisher's Cataloging-In-Publication Data

Names: Lewkowicz, Freda, author. | Benjamin, Siona, illustrator.
Title: I am Hava : a song's story of love, hope & joy / written by Freda Lewkowicz ; illustrated by Siona Benjamin.
Description: First edition. | Seattle, WA : Intergalactic Afikoman, [2021] | Interest age level: 004-010. | Summary: "The story of the world's most famous Jewish song, as told by the song herself"-- Provided by publisher.
Identifiers: ISBN 9781951365066
Subjects: LCSH: Havah nagilah--Juvenile fiction. | Songs, Hebrew--Juvenile fiction. | Jews--Music--Juvenile fiction. | CYAC: Havah nagilah--Fiction. | Songs, Hebrew--Fiction. | Jews--Music--Fiction.
Classification: LCC PZ7.1.L522 Ia 2021 | DDC [E]--dc23

Library of Congress Control Number: 2021938408
Printed in the USA
First Edition
2 4 6 8 10 9 7 5 3 1

I AM HAVA

A Song's Story of Love, Hope & Joy

Written by FREDA LEWKOWICZ

Illustrated by SIONA BENJAMIN

I was born a niggun, a melody without words.

I spread hope and joy even in times of trouble.

That was my mitzvah.

My life began in Sadagora, a small shtetl in Ukraine.

All week long, the keepers of my melody studied Torah quietly.

On Shabbat and Jewish holidays,
they hummed my melody joyously.
Their black coats swayed as they sang.
Their hands pounded the tish.
Their voices boomed.

But danger surrounded us.

And so we sailed.
Oh, how we suffered
on the voyage.

Filth. Hunger. Disease. Thirst.

"What have we done?"
we cried as the steamship
rocked in angry seas.

“Sh’ma Yisrael,” we prayed.
“Hear, O Israel, the Lord our God, the Lord is One.”

Finally, we arrived in Jerusalem.
For 2000 years, we were like seeds
scattered everywhere around the world.

But now we were home.

"Someday, when my words find me,
I'll sing a love song to this moment."

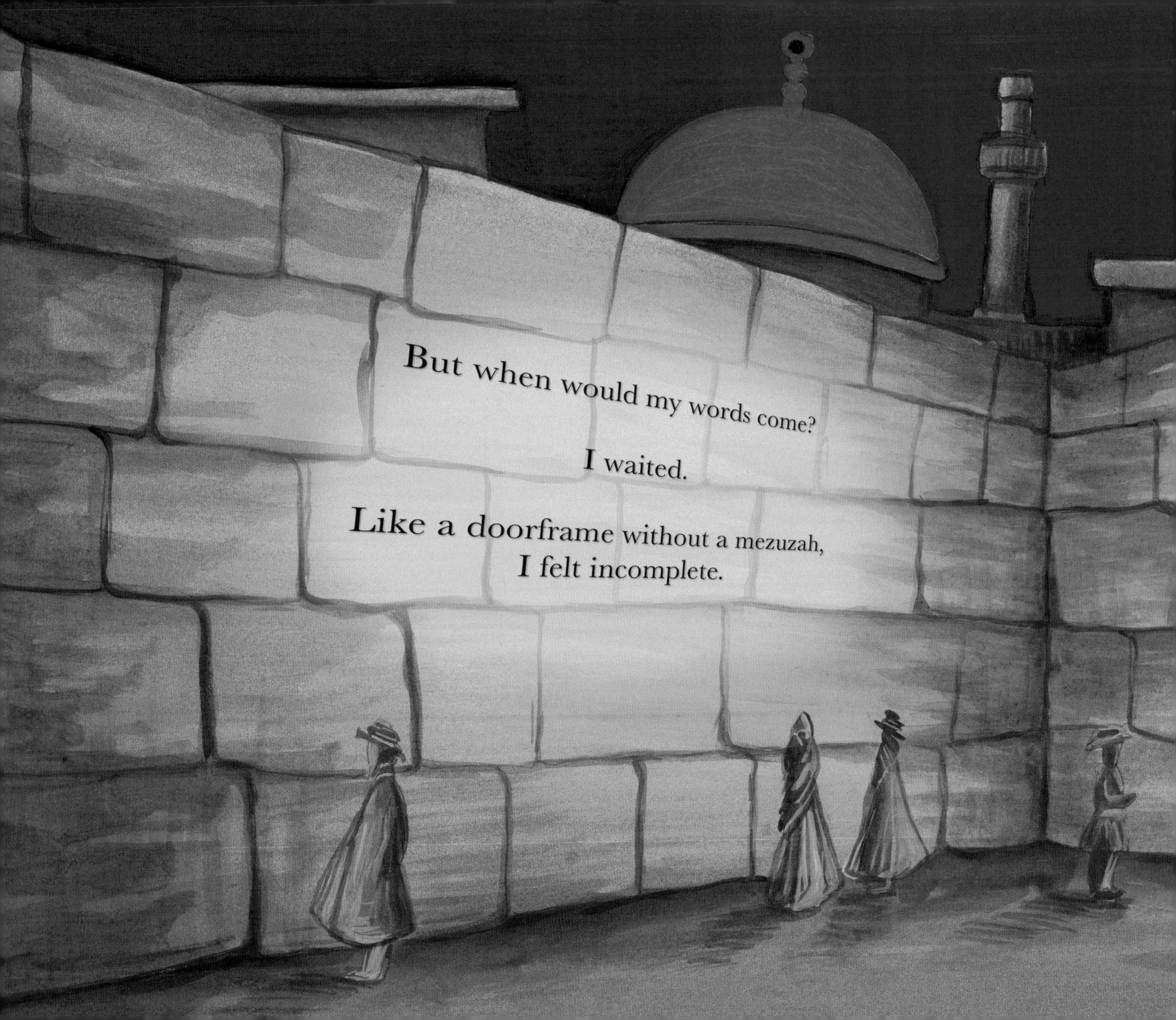

But when would my words come?

I waited.

Like a doorframe without a mezuzah,
I felt incomplete.

I sang my wish to
the cracks of the Kotel.

"Hashem. I dedicate myself to the mitzvah of spreading joy. Please send my words."

Finally, my prayers were answered.
Abraham Zvi Idelsohn, a musicologist,
searched for the perfect melody to celebrate.

My joyous tune dazzled him.

I became HAVA NAGILA, meaning COME AND REJOICE.

Until today, my true lyricist remains a mystery.

“Who wrote Hava Naglila?
Was it Abraham Zvi Idelsohn
or his student, Moshe
Nathanson?”
they ask me.

“My words are a miracle, a gift from Hashem,” I answer.

Oh, the power of my new Hebrew words.
Spinning. Whirling. Swooping. Celebrating.

"Let us celebrate," my music urged.
"Forget worries and enemies.

Forget the difficulty of a
new life in a new country."

Then came HORA.

It felt electric when the passion of my song joined the power and vibrant energy of her dance.

When Israel was founded, the new country danced
and celebrated with us in endless circles of light,

and then Hora and I danced across the ocean… together.

Today, I celebrate at weddings,
bat mitzvahs and bar mitzvahs.

I thundered at Carnegie Hall
with Harry Belafonte.

I took a bow in movies.
Artists recorded me
hundreds of times.

I am as Jewish as chicken soup,
but I float across borders,
religions and cultures.
Soccer fans in Amsterdam bellow my words.

Lena Horne sang her civil rights anthem "Now!" to my melody.

In London, at the 2012 Olympics, Aly Raisman
twirled, tumbled, leaped and won the gold to my melody

Hardships disappear when people clap and sing my words:

Hava nagila, hava nagila

Hava nagila ve'nismeḥa

Hava neranena, hava neranena

Hava neranena ve'nismeḥa

Uru, uru aḥim

Uru aḥim be'lev sameaḥ

Come and rejoice.

Come and rejoice and be happy.

Come and sing, sing and be happy.

Wake up, my brothers,
with a happy heart.

I invite you to SING.

I invite you to DANCE.

I invite you to STOMP
and spin and soar.

I settle softly on the world and blanket it with hope.
This is my mitzvah.
Yes, I am Hava Nagila.

I am JOY.

FREDA LEWKOWICZ was born in Montreal, Quebec, where her parents, both Holocaust survivors, settled after the war. She is the author of *School Selfies: Teachers, Parents, Students and Bandwagons* and *Oliver Soliver,* illustrated by Felipe Huarnez. A graduate of Concordia and McGill universities, she lives in Cote St. Luc, Quebec, with her husband. To learn more about Freda, please visit fredalewkowicz.com.

Growing up as a Bene Israel Jew in multicultural India, **SIONA BENJAMIN** read Disney comics, Enid Blyton children's novels and Amar Chitra comic books about Indian mythology. In her paintings, Siona combines the imagery of her past with the role she plays in America today, making a mosaic inspired by both Indian miniature paintings and transcultural mythology. Siona is a two-time Fulbright fellowship winner and has two MFA degrees in painting and theater set design. Her work has been featured in publications including *The New York Times*, *The Chicago Tribune*, *The Financial Times*, *The Boston Globe*, *The Times of India*, *ArtNews* and *The Jerusalem Post.* Today Siona lives in New Jersey, and her work has been exhibited in galleries and museums in India, the US and Israel. She is the subject of a documentary titled *Blue Like Me* and a book titled *Growing Up Jewish in India: From the Bene Israel to the Art of Siona Benjamin.* You can learn more about Siona and her art at www.artsiona.com.

AUTHOR'S NOTE

My Personal Connection to Hava Nagila

My parents were living in Hasenhecke DP (Displaced Persons') Camp in Germany in 1948.

Not long before, cattle cars, powered by hatred, had rumbled through Europe. Safe now, my parents were displaced persons. "Displaced," as if someone had simply lost them. Like other Holocaust survivors, they were broken and in mourning. Yet the joyful sounds of Hava Nagila sometimes echoed in the camp. "Let us celebrate," it urged. The song symbolized hope and resilience. Yes, the survivors could rebuild their lives, filled with the scars of memory but also overflowing with glorious freedoms. The astounding rate of weddings and births in the DP camps reveal this belief in a future. Singing and dancing and listening to Hava Nagila allowed my parents to believe that they could weave the threads of a new life in a new world.

Sometimes, simple things like a song called Hava Nagila have great healing power. Even in Hasenhecke DP Camp in 1948.

To learn more about Hava Nagila, including a detailed timeline and bibliography, please visit www.IntergalacticAfikoman.com.

ILLUSTRATOR'S NOTE

Why Is Hava Blue?

For me, Hava's story is a story of universality and multiculturalism. Universality is always born from the specifics. The specifics for me are my Jewishness, my Indianness and my Americanness.

Many blue-skinned characters populate my paintings. Hava is blue because blue is the color of the sky and the ocean. Blue is the color of the globe. Blue is also such a Jewish color. It's in the tallit. It's in the tzitzit. It's in the Israeli flag.

Hava is blue because she is Jewish and she is universal. She belongs everywhere and nowhere at the same time.

Yad Vashem Photo Archive, Jerusalem. 1486_302

November 1947, Jews dancing in the Hasenhecke DP camp